Anonymous

Sweet Story of Old

Anonymous

Sweet Story of Old

ISBN/EAN: 9783337332129

Printed in Europe, USA, Canada, Australia, Japan

Cover: Foto ©Andreas Hilbeck / pixelio.de

More available books at **www.hansebooks.com**

THE SWEET STORY OF OLD

THE SWEET STORY OF OLD.

"FEED MY LAMBS."
St. John xxi. 15.

LONDON:

THE RELIGIOUS TRACT SOCIETY;

56, PATERNOSTER-ROW, AND 164, PICCADILLY;

AND SOLD BY THE BOOKSELLERS.

1861.

CONTENTS.

JERUSALEM.

I. TELL ME ABOUT JESUS.

"TELL ME ABOUT JESUS." So said a little boy to a lady who had called to see him.

The dear child's mamma was dead, and he now lived with a kind aunt, who was very fond of him.

The lady had taken him on her lap, to talk to him. Among other things she had told him a story out of the Bible about Jesus, the Son of God. As soon as he heard the name, he sprang on his feet with joy in his face, and cried, " Oh ! please *do* tell me about Jesus."

" Tell you about Jesus ? " said the lady. "Yes, my dear child, I cannot better speak of any one than he. We ought often to talk about him."

He then sat on her lap again, while the lady spoke to him of the birth, the life, and the death of our Lord Jesus Christ. She told of his great love to children, and

of the kind words he spoke to them.
You may be sure she did not
forget those spoken by Jesus when
mothers came with their little ones
to him: "Suffer little children,
and forbid them not, to come unto
me; for of such is the kingdom of
heaven."*

When she had done talking,
the child threw his arms round
her neck, and kissed her a good
many times.

Why did he wish her to speak
in this way? "Before dear

* Matthew xix. 14.

mamma went away," said he, " she often told me about Jesus. And when mamma had told me all, she used to kneel down alone with me, and hold me by the hand. Then she used to whisper to Jesus." He meant that she used to pray very softly.

" But when mamma had gone, she never came back. I have no one now to talk to me, and to kiss me as she did."

That night, the lady sat by the side of his bed, and told the aunt of what the little boy had said.

It was found that he had often spoken to his aunt in the same way.   But she said that she did not know how to talk to children.

The little boy lay asleep with one of his tiny hands under his cheek, and a smile upon his pale face.   The aunt looked at him, and felt that she loved him very much.   " I will try," she said, " to speak to him as his mamma used to do.   If I try, God will help me to speak in a way that may do good to my dear boy."

A few weeks after this time, he was taken very ill. Day after day his aunt folded him in her arms, and told him of some kind deed that Jesus did, or some blessed word he spoke. Then the child would put his hands round her neck and kiss her, saying, "Tell me *more* about Jesus."

The little boy did not live long, for he was taken to dwell in heaven. After he was gone, his aunt often went to his grave. As she stood by its side she wept. And in her heart she said, " I will from this time try to tell dear little ones of the love of Jesus. It shall be my delight to lead them to him of whom my sweet child loved so much to hear."

It was not long after this before the aunt was a teacher in a Sunday-school ; and many little ones heard her tell of " the sweet story of old."

Dear young reader, are you ready to say with this little boy, " Tell *me* about Jesus ?" Then read this book. It has been written for you. You may find in it some words of truth and love which may do you good.

There are some tales that are not true. They are about what might have taken place. They tell of little boys and girls who never lived. Yet they are true in one sense, for these children are very much like some children who have lived in the world. Those who wrote the stories made them out of their own minds. Perhaps they did not wish us to think that they are true. But they wrote them to teach us good and wise lessons.

There are other stories that are foolish. They only amuse us. They do us no real good. We are not better or wiser after we have read them than we were before.

The Holy Bible is full of stories. They are all true, wise, and good. One is of the babe Moses in his little ark of rushes. Another is of the child Samuel in the Temple of God. Then there is the story of young David killing the Giant; and one of pious Josiah, who was a king when only eight years old. Nor must we forget the little captive maid, whose words led her rich master to the prophet of God.

It is hoped that you will always love to read all these stories and other blessed things in the book of God itself.

But the best story is about our Lord Jesus Christ.   Though all cannot be told you now, you will be glad to hear a part of it.

The story is not a new one, yet it never seems to be old.   Little children who lived long ago, used to listen to it with joy.   There are many who are now alive, who have read it many times, yet they love to read it again and again. They say it suits them now, though they have grown to be quite old. Other little girls and boys will listen to it and read it when you have passed away from this world. And in heaven it will be as a "new song" for ever and ever.

There are some pretty verses, which a lady wrote for little children. Perhaps you know them by heart, and can sing them. Come, let us listen to them again.

I think, when I read that sweet story of old,
   When Jesus dwelt here among men,
And call'd little children as lambs to his fold,
   I should like to have been with them then.

I wish that his hands had been put on my
      head,
   And that I had been placed on his knee,
And that I might have seen his kind look
      when he said,
   " Let the little ones come unto me."

Yet still to my Saviour in prayer I may go,
   And ask for a share in his love ;
And if I thus earnestly seek him below,
   I shall see him and hear him above :

In that beautiful place he's gone to prepare
   For all who are wash'd and forgiven ;
And many dear children are gathering there,
   " For of such is the kingdom of heaven."

BETHLEHEM.

II. THE NAME JESUS.

THE Son of God dwelt in heaven before the world was made. He ever lived there. He will always live there. He is "over all God blessed for ever."

But he took upon him our nature. In that nature he was born into this world. He came as a child like you; and yet not like you. He had the nature and body of a child; but he was

c

not born in sin. He was the "holy Child"—quite holy—always holy.

When the angel came to the Virgin Mary, and told her that she should be the mother of the blessed Child, the angel said that his name was to be JESUS.

In that place in the Bible in which this is told us,* there is no reason given for calling the Child by this name. But in another place,† it is said that when the angel came to Joseph, the husband

---

* Luke i. 31.   † Matthew i. 21.

of Mary, and made this thing known unto him, he gave this reason for naming the child: "For he shall save his people from their sins."

Jesus was a right name to give to a child that was to be the Saviour of the world. It means the very same as Saviour.

In those days people used to give to their children names that might tell something about them. And many of the names we give to infants now have a meaning. David means "beloved;" Job, "he that weeps;" John, "the gift of the Lord;" Sarah, "a princess;" and Mary, "exalted."

A German father called his little son by the name of Gott-hold, because God had been very kind to the family, and they were thankful to him. *Gott* means "God;" and *hold* means "mild" or "kind." They wanted to have their child's name remind them how very kind God had been to them.

We have said that Jesus is a Saviour. Whom did he come to

save ? It was to save sinners that he came ; to save every one who trusts in him and loves him ; to save you if you will do so.

You know what sin is. All evil deeds, and all bad words, and all wrong thoughts, and all naughty tempers, are sin. When children do not speak the truth, but tell lies, they sin. When they are in a passion, or are sullen, or selfish, they sin. When they do not obey their parents, they sin against God.

Every little child has a heart

from which sins are as sure to come as sparks from burning wood. They have a sinful nature. They do what they ought not to do, and leave undone what they ought to do. Satan, the wicked spirit, also seeks to lead them into sin.

All people who have lived in the world were lost sinners. But Jesus " came to seek and to save the lost." This is why all who love him may call him *our* Saviour.

A girl was at play by the side of a river. As she ran along, her foot slipped, and she fell into the water. She would have been drowned had not a man jumped into the river. He caught her by the hand, and swam with her to the shore. He saved her from drowning.

As a man rode on a horse through a forest, on a dark night, he heard a cry. It was like the cry of a little child. He stopped, and then he heard it again. He was not quite sure that it was a child, for he knew that some wild beasts often make a noise like a child's cry. Now, if he should go to the place, and it should be a tiger or a panther, he might be torn to death. But if it were a child lost in the forest, and if he should go on and not try to find it, then the poor child might be starved, or be eaten up by the wild beasts. Its mother would never again see her dear child.

The man was kind and brave ; and as the sad cry kept coming to his ears, he made up his mind what to do. He sprang from his horse, tied it to a tree, and went slowly in the dark to the spot whence the sound came. He walked a little way, and then stopped to listen. Then he went a little further, and stopped again. As he walked among the trees, he felt something touch his knee, and a soft voice said, "Dear papa, is it you?"

Yes; there was the lost child —a little boy. He had strayed away from his father's house, in search of wild roses.

The kind man took him in his arms. When he got to his horse

again, he put the little boy in front on the saddle. After a while he saw a light. When he came to it, what place do you think it was? It was the home of the child. His father and mother had been seeking for him for two days. They had said, " We shall never see our boy any more;" and then they wept. But, oh, with what joy did they now take him to their arms! Thus the man saved the child that was lost.

Jesus came as the Good Shepherd, to seek the sheep that were lost. It was said of him more than seven hundred years before he came into the world, that he would "gather the lambs with his arm, and carry them in his bosom."*

If you were to see a shepherd now, in the lands where the Bible was written, you would better know what is meant by these words. There the shepherd still carries the tender lambs, and goes before the sheep. He feeds them, and is kind to them. If any one

* Isaiah xl. 11.

wanders, and is lost, he seeks till he finds it. When he has found it, he carries it back to the fold. You may now look at the picture, and see such a shepherd.

How does Jesus save ?   In this way.   He saw that we were lost in sin.   He knew that if he did not save us, we must for ever perish.   To save us, he came into the world.   He lived and died for us.   The Bible says that Jesus "died for our sins."*

* 1 Cor. xv. 3

AN EASTERN SHEPHERD

Jesus obeyed the law of his Father. He kept every command. In him was no sin. It was for us he obeyed. For us, too, he bore great sorrow and pain. He wore a crown of thorns, and was nailed to a cross of wood, for us. He was wounded for our sins. He laid down his life to save us. He suffered that those who believe in him might not suffer. Greater love he could not have shown than by laying down his life, that he might save sinners.

Jesus came to save both body

and soul.   The man who saved
the little girl from being drowned,
only saved the body.   So he who
found the little boy in the forest,
only saved the body from death.
But Jesus came to save both soul
and body.

It was, also, to save us from sin
itself that Jesus came.   He came
to save from its power over us,
and from the love of sin in us.
For this he gives his Holy Spirit,
to make us holy.   If we are not
made holy, we cannot go to heaven.
He gives a new heart, to love and

obey God. If we have not this new heart, we cannot live with God in heaven.

Think, then, how great was the love of Jesus, to do all this for those who have sinned. And his love is still as great as it ever was. He says, "Come unto me, and be saved." He speaks to us now : "Come, I am able. Come, I am willing. Come, I am waiting."

Listen, then, to his words. If you are a very little child, go to Jesus, for he will not turn away from those who are young in

years.   Are you a poor child?
Go to Jesus; he will look in
love on the poorest child on earth.
Are you an afflicted child?   Go
to Jesus; he was once afflicted
too.   Are you an orphan child?
Do you say that your dear father
or mother is dead?   Go to Jesus:
he will pity you, and be better to
you than any earthly parent can
be.

It will never be more easy for
you to go to Jesus than it is now.
Then hear his kind words, and be
happy.

NAZARETH.

III. THE HOLY CHILD JESUS.

A GREAT many years ago, a large crowd was seen in the land of the Jews. They were on their way home from the great city of that people. A feast had been kept there, called the feast of Passover.

God had told the Jews to keep this feast.* It was to remind them of the night when their fathers

* Exodus xii. 3—17.

were *passed over* by the angel
who slew the first-born of Egypt.
At such a time the people from all
parts of the land went up to the
city to keep the feast.   It was to
them a season of great joy.

Those who came from distant
towns were on the road some
days.   They rested under the
shade of trees or rocks when the
sun's heat was great.   In the cool
of the day they went on their
way.

The Pass-over was kept at a
time of the year when the fruit

had begun to appear on the fig and olive trees, and the vines had put forth their young grapes. Roses then bloomed on the sides of the hills, and sweet lilies peeped out in the corners of the valleys.

It must have been a pretty sight when the people rested at night by the side of a well. Do you not think you can see them? Look how they set up their tents, and spread their cloaks on the ground for beds. They sit down to their supper. Now they sing

a sweet hymn, and then they say
their evening prayer. Soon they
are all at rest, and the full bright
moon shines above them in the
sky.

Among these people is Mary
the mother of Jesus. She has
been up to the feast with her
husband Joseph, and her son, who
is now about twelve years old. As
they return, her son is not at her
side, but she thinks that he is
along with some of her friends in
the company.*

* Luke ii. 41—52.

But when night comes on, she seeks for her boy. She asks her friends if they have seen him. No ; he has not been seen on the road. He is not to be found among the travellers.

Other parents have their children quite safe, and close the day in peace and joy. But where can the son of Mary be ? Has any one seen her son Jesus ? He had never done anything to sadden her heart, for he had always obeyed her word. He was all that a mother's heart could wish a child to be. She could trust him at all times, but what had now become of him? She must go back, and seek for him on the road and in the city.

One day passes away, but Mary has not found her son. Two days are gone, and yet he is still lost. At last she comes to the Temple, and hastens up its broad steps, and through its wide doors; and there is her son, sitting with some of the doctors, or learned men. He is both hearing them and asking them questions.

These wise men are full of wonder as they find the child so ready to listen to their words, and so quick to learn every truth they speak.

When his mother told him that she and Joseph had sought him in sorrow, he said that he must be about the business of his Father. He had come into this world to do the work of God. It was not an idle wish to break away from his mother, or to take things into his own hands. It was a desire to do what was right, and to obey

God: for he once said, "I do always
the things that please him."*

But because he had to do a
great work for God, did he refuse
to go home with his mother? Oh
no ; he knew that it was right to
obey her.   He then went back to
her house, and was " subject unto
her."

Mary his mother, and Joseph,
who stood in the place of an earthly
father, were sinners. Jesus was
without sin, yet he obeyed them.
They were human, and he was

* John viii. 29.

God as well as man ; yet he was
subject unto them. Though he
was so wise, and great, and good,
he did what they told him to do,
and he did all in a meek and
loving spirit.

Jesus was called "the car-
penter's son."* Do you think,
that when he was young, he lived
an idle life? Do you suppose
that he strolled over the hills, and
along the fields, or sat at home,
and did nothing to help his mother

* Matthew xiii. 55.

and Joseph? Even rich Jews made their sons learn a trade. So that, if the sons became poor, they might be able to work for their living. But Mary and Joseph were poor. They had to toil for their bread: you may be sure, then, that Jesus helped them, and that he spent the days of his youth in a useful and busy way. He has taught us that common work, if it be honest work, is no disgrace.

Jesus loved his mother all the days he was on the earth. He

showed her honour to the last. Oh, what love was that which grew day by day between that mother and her son!

About twenty years after he first went to the great city, he went there for the last time. It is not said that Mary went with him; but we suppose she did, for she *was* there. When he was nailed to the cross, and all his disciples had left him but John, his mother did not leave him. She stood near him in his great pain. And in the midst of his

sorrow he did not forget her. He
said to John, "Behold thy mother." As if he had told him,
"Be to her as a son; look to her
as a mother. Take care of her
as long as she lives." And John
did so; for "from that hour he
took her to his own home."* Thus
Jesus loved his mother to the
last.

Dear child, who may now read
this book, do you love to learn
what is good, and seek to be wise

* John xix. 25—27.

in the things of God? Do you
ask questions about the truths that
are in the Holy Bible, and listen
to what is said to you? You will
do so, if you wish to be like Jesus.

Do you try to please your parents? Do you mind them in
little as well as in great things?
Yes, if you are like Jesus.

Will those who grow up to talk
with the great and wise listen
to the words of their parents?
Will they never by speech or conduct bring sorrow to their hearts?
When their parents have grown

old, or have become ill, will they still obey and honour them ? To be sure they will, if they have the same mind as was in Jesus.

Think of these things.

A party of little girls and boys stood talking on the village green. They were about to spend a half-holiday in the woods. Wild flowers—red, white, and blue— were to be made into little crowns and put on their heads. Oh, it was a nice happy time they hoped to have in the woods.

"Now, dear Ellen," said Susan Jones, "run home, and ask your mother if you may go with us. Tell her we are all going, and that you must go too." Ellen skipped across the road, and soon was in her mother's cottage. She was gone some time.

The little party waited for her, and when she came slowly walking towards them, they cried, "You have got leave, Ellen; have you not?" Ellen shook her head, and said that her mother could not spare her. "Oh, do come;

E

you must go," shouted some of the children.

Then Ellen tried to look happy, and meekly said, " My mother knows best." That was right, Ellen. Obey and honour your mother, and it will save you from many tears and sorrows.

You can now read another true story of a little girl who wished to be like Jesus. It is thus told by one who loves children.

I am very sure if you had known my young friend Minka

you would have loved her.   It is
a great many years ago when I
met her for the first and only time,
but it seems as if I could still
hear her soft voice, and see her
smiling face.

Minka was born in the cold
snowy land called Russia.   It
pleased God to take her dear
mother away from her when she
was quite a child.   But she had a
kind father, who was a nobleman,
and very rich.

As her father loved Jesus, he
felt a wish to spend his money

in doing good.   He had school-
houses built on his estates for
children, and Bibles were freely
given to their fathers and mothers.

Two or three years after the
death of her mother, Minka went
with her father a long journey.
It was to visit some pious friends
in Switz-er-land.

Little Minka dearly loved her
father. She tried in every way she
could to obey him. One lovely
day, when the flowers filled the
air with their sweet smell, she was
at a house where there were a

good many ladies and gentlemen. There were also present some children of her own age, with whom she could talk ; for Minka had learned to speak English and French very well.

It was soon time for tea, and Minka's father was at the top of the table, and she was at the other end.   A gentleman sat next to her, and was much pleased with her gentle, modest ways.   He hoped she was a good child. Soon he found that she was so, for she not only obeyed her parent, but feared God.

There was on the table some nice sweet honey. The comb was white as silver, and was running over with its sweet honey. The gentleman who sat by Minka asked her to taste it. As he thought she might be timid in not taking some, he put a piece of it on her plate.

"Minka," said he, "you have never tasted such honey. It is got by Swiss bees from Swiss flowers on the high hills. Do eat some : it will not hurt you."

But Minka did not touch it.

She asked that the tempting bit of sweet should not be placed on her plate. And looking up with her blue eyes, she said, "Please, sir, do not give me any. I do not wish to have it."

"Why, Minka, do you not like honey? All the little girls whom I know like it. Have the children in Russia no taste for that which is sweet?"

"Oh, I like it much, sir; but my papa says it is not good for me, and I am not to touch it."

The gentleman was struck by

what she said; and he thought
he would further try her. He
should not have done so. It was
not right to tempt the little girl.
But we shall see how firm and
brave she was.

"Your father," said he, "will
not know that you have had any
honey. I will only let you taste
it. Let me give you this very
small bit."

Now what do you think the
little Russian girl did? Did she
take it, or did she not?

Minka calmly looked up, and

fixed her eyes on the gentleman. Then in a very modest way she replied, " But God sees me, sir, and he will know it."

As I have already said, I never saw Minka after that time. Her father soon went back to Russia, and Minka with him. But often do I think of that dear girl, and hope that she grew up to be strong in the fear and love of God.

Will you, young reader, ask God to give you his grace, that you may be like the little girls of

whom you have now read?   But
more than all, will you not try
to be like Jesus?

Oh! why did not the Son of God
  Come as an angel bright?
And why not leave his fair abode
  To come with power and might?

Because he came not here to reign
  As king and prince below;
He came to save our souls from sin,
  Whence all our sorrows flow.

Accept, O ever-blessed Lord,
  An infant's humble praise;
Teach me to love thy holy word,
  And serve thee all my days.

BETHESDA.

IV. JESUS WENT ABOUT DOING GOOD.

HE THE SICK TO HEALTH RESTORED ;
TO THE POOR HE PREACHED HIS WORD ;
AND LET LITTLE CHILDREN SHARE
IN HIS LOVE AND TENDER CARE.

JESUS had no home to call his own. Foxes had holes, and birds flew to their soft nests, but he had not where to lay his head. If you had seen him, you would have known how poor he was for our sake.

He who was the Maker of all worlds came, not to be served, but

to serve. The Lord of angels
came not to be waited on as a
master, but to wait on others as a
servant. He did not seek to
please himself. He was ready to
give up his own ease and rest,
that he might make men happy.

But though so poor, no one
ever did so much good as he did.
He did good at all times, in all
places, and to all kinds of people.
It was his delight to do good.

Jesus did not sit down in some
quiet spot, and wait for the people
to come to him; He "went about"

the streets of the city, and did good there. Then he passed into the green lanes and fields and villages, and did good there. He walked by the side of the sea, and did good there. When the sun was hot, or the storm blew, or the roads were bad, he did not stop in his work of mercy. When he was tired, and hungry, and thirsty, he was ready to help all who were in any trouble.

Let us see some of the ways in which Jesus did good.

There are some people who lose

the use of their limbs. They cannot walk or move about. They lie in a helpless state for many years, and are often full of pain. When Jesus was on the earth, many such poor men and women were made well by him.

As he went up one day to the Temple, he saw a man lying by the side of a pool of water. The place was called the "house of mercy." He had lost the use of his limbs for thirty-eight years. That you know is a very long time indeed.

This pool had been as a house of mercy to many. God was pleased at times to send an angel to trouble, or move the waters. Then the first person who stepped in upon the moving of the waters was made well. Only one was cured at a time.

The poor man had seen others who had lain at his side made well. He had seen them go to their homes with joy. Did he not hope that some day he too might be cured?

Jesus looked in pity at this poor

F

man, and asked, " Wilt thou be
made whole?" Why, this was
what he had long waited for; but
he had no kind friends to help
him to the waters when the angel
came to move them. But as
there was so kind a look in him
who spoke, the man told his sad
tale.

He had not now long to wait;
for Jesus said, " Rise, take up
thy bed, and walk." He who
spoke the word gave the power.
And at once he stood up, and
soon, rolling up the bed or carpet

on which he lay, he went to his own house.*

A father once came to Jesus. " I have brought unto thee my son," said he, " who hath a dumb spirit. O Lord, look upon him, for he is my only child." The father went on to tell his great sorrow. His son, in the bloom of youth, had lost his reason. Instead of being a comfort to his parents, he was a cause of care and distress. Sometimes he fell

* John v. 1—16.

into the fire, and at other times into the water; so that his life was always in danger. Nor could the poor child tell what he felt, for he was deaf and dumb. And what was worse than all, an evil spirit was in him.

"Lord, have mercy on my son," cried the father. Jesus turned and told him to bring the poor boy to him. And as they brought him, the unclean spirit cast him on the ground, where he lay tearing his body, and foaming at his mouth.

Was not this a very sad case? But it was to show the power of Jesus over wicked spirits, and the love of his heart for those who are sick.

Jesus knew what he could do, and what he would do. He said, "Thou deaf and dumb spirit, come out of him." And at once the spirit came forth. Then he took the boy by the hand and lifted him up. He was no longer a deaf and dumb child, and under the power of the devil, but quite well and free.*

* Mark ix. 14—29.

Do you not hope that the first use he made of his ears was to listen to the words of Jesus, and that his new gift of speech was used to thank and praise him? Yes, we will hope so.

When some people see a sick man they turn away. We know that Jesus did not. He was ready not only to speak kind words, but to help and heal. He showed his pity in deeds. We will see it in another case.

A rich man had a little girl,

about twelve years old. She was
very ill, and at the point of death.
He had heard of the wonders
Jesus had done, and as his last
hope went to him.

Do you not think you see him,
as he goes to the place where
Jesus was? It may be that he
said in his own mind, " He healed
a rich man's son. He raised up
the servant of another. He
cured the poor man at the pool.
To those blind men he gave sight,
and that deaf and dumb boy he
made quite well. I will try what

he can do for me.   Will he not
hear me, also, when I ask him to
help my dear girl?"

When the father met Jesus, he
told him his errand.   And Jesus
went with him.   As they came to
the house where the young child
lay, the people ran from the door,
and said, "She is dead."

Oh, what did the father then
feel?   He thought that help had
come too late.   As soon as Jesus
heard the word that was spoken,
he said, "Be not afraid; only believe, and she shall be made whole."

The rich man was soon to see that Jesus had as much power over the dead as over the living.

Our Lord went into the room where the body of the young maiden lay, and stood by its side. He took hold of her hand, and called on her to arise. The words were no sooner spoken, than the soul came back to the body. The glow of health was again on her cheeks, and she arose as if only awoke out of sleep.*

Did this little girl live to be

* Mark v. 22—24, 35—43.

old ?   Did she become one of
those who loved Jesus ?   Did she
follow him all the days of her life ?
We do not know, and yet we may
trust that she did become one of
the holy women who obeyed his
word.

One day Jesus was seen on the
road which led to the city of Nain.
Had any one sent for him ?   No ;
he knew there was a work of
mercy to be done, and he was
going to do it.

As he came near to the city,

the people slowly bore the body of a young man, to lay it in the grave. A mother had lost her only son. She had no husband to comfort her, for he, too, was dead.

Jesus saw her tears. He drew nigh to her, and said, "Weep not." He knew all about her trouble, and he meant to turn her sorrow into joy. "Young man," he said, "I say unto thee, Arise." Then he that was dead sat up, and began to speak; and Jesus took him by the hand, and gave

him to his mother.   And what a
gift was that—her son, her only
child, folded in her arms again!

Who can tell what the young
man felt as he started into life from
the dead ?   Who can tell the joy
of the mother as she felt the warm
kiss of her son again ?   Jesus
saw the delight he had given, and
went on his way to other works of
mercy.*

It is a very sad case when any
one cannot see the bright sky and

* Luke vii. 11—17.

the sweet roses and lilies, and the faces of those he loves. Pity the poor blind. Jesus always pitied them.

Two poor blind men were by the way-side, and heard the noise of the people as they ran along the road. Who is coming? Oh! good news; it is Jesus. When the blind men heard who it was, they cried aloud, "Thou Son of David, have mercy on us."

There were some in the crowd who told them to "hold their peace." But they called the

that sight had been given them in
answer to their faith and prayer.*

There were many more such
kind deeds as these which Jesus
did.   His life was full of them.
He cured the people without
delay, without pain, and without
money.   No wonder, then, that
they went to him.

Do you think that he cured
these because they were holy and
good people?   No; they were
sinners as we all are.   They were

* Matthew xx. 30—34.

not better than others. It was
his great love that led him to be
so kind.

Did not every one love him
because he was so full of love to
them? No; only a few loved
him. Wicked men called him
bad names. They cast him out
from their cities. They mocked
him, and in every way were cruel
to him. Yet he bore it all, for he
loved them still. We love those
who love us. Jesus loved those
who hated him.

WELL AT CANA.

"SUFFER LITTLE CHILDREN, AND FORBID THEM NOT, TO COME UNTO ME; FOR OF SUCH IS THE KINGDOM OF HEAVEN."—*Matt.* xix. 14.

THE heart of Jesus was so full of love, that we should have been quite sure he loved little children, even if we had not been told so. One so kind and gentle as he was, would not turn away from them.

But we are plainly told that Jesus cares for children. Rich or poor, he loves them. He does not wish them to be lost. He

desires that they should be saved.
Here, then, is good news for you
—for all the little ones.

Should you like to see a picture
of some children who came to
Jesus? It is not such a picture
as you may have seen, where a
sort of likeness is given of our
Lord. We are not told in the
Bible who or what he was like.
There may be a reason why we
should not know. We might bow
before a picture, and honour
that, instead of the Saviour himself.

We cannot tell how he looked, and we will not make a picture of that kind. But we will give a word - picture, taken from the Bible, and therefore true.

A crowd is seen on the road to the Temple, in the great city of the Jews. The people are told that the holy Teacher, Jesus, is on his way, and they go out to meet him.

When they see him they put him on an ass. As they go along the crowd becomes very great. Some spread their clothes on the

ground. Others cut down branches
from the trees, and lay them on
the road.

We think we hear the people
say, " Who is this?" And now
a loud shout is heard, " Hosanna
to the Son of David. Blessed is
he that cometh in the name of
the Lord." The word Hosanna
means, " Lord, save, we pray
thee."

But now another cry is heard.
It is the sweet voices of children.
They stop in their play, and begin
to shout " Hosanna," too ;

Nor does their zeal offend him ;
But, as he rides along,
He lets them still attend him,
And listens to their song.

Jesus now goes into the Temple; and it is not long before the blind and the lame hear that he is in the holy place. Soon their cry for pity and help is heard. Nor do they call on him in vain. In his great love he makes them quite well. You may be sure that there is much joy among all the people who have come to the place, when they see what is done. And now again the children who have

come to the Temple cry "Hosanna."

The priests try to stop the songs
of the little ones. They say to
Jesus, "Hearest thou what these
say?" And Jesus replies, "Yea,
have ye never read, Out of the
mouths of babes and sucklings
thou hast perfected praise?"

It may be that some of these
little ones do as other people do.
They do not quite know what they
mean when they cry aloud; like
some now who sing the praises of
God, but do not mind the words

they use.   Yet we think some of
them may know.   It is as if they
say, "We are glad that the Saviour has come. Save us, O Lord.
Welcome to the Son of David."*

Young reader, you cannot do
as these little children did.   But
you can go to the house of God,
and praise him there.   You can
there sing with your heart as well
as with your voice.

The children of whom you have
just read CAME to Jesus.   There

* Matthew xxi. 12—16 ; Luke xix. 35—41.

were others who were BROUGHT to
him. They may have been too
young to have gone alone. Their
mothers took them by the hand,
or carried them in their arms.

The account in the Bible of
those who were thus brought is
very short, but it is full of hope
and promise for the little ones.
We love to call it the "SWEET
STORY OF OLD."

Jesus with loving words and
kind looks is teaching the people,
and doing good to their bodies.
Just at this time some proud men

come to ask him many things.
They do not wish to be taught, but
they hope to stop Jesus in his work.

While they are speaking, there
is a stir among the crowd.   Who
are they who push and try to
get forward ?   They are mothers
and others who wish to get
near the good Teacher.   What
do they want ?   It is a great
matter that has brought them here.
They have come with their little
children that Jesus may "touch
them."*   They have come to ask

* Mark x. 13.

him to put his hands on their
infants, and pray for them.*

We may suppose that the parents have seen what the touch of
Jesus can do. And they know
that laying the hands on the head
is a very old custom. When this
is done, they hope that a blessing
will rest on their dear little ones.

Are the disciples glad when
they see these children brought to
their Master? No; they are
angry. They may think that
Jesus will not notice these babes.

* Matthew xix. 13.

Or they may suppose that he will not be troubled about them just at this time. That he is too busy, and cannot attend to children. He is now talking to wise men—perhaps old men — why come now?

How strange it is that they should so think! They do not wait to see what Jesus will do, but they begin to rebuke those who have brought the children.

But Jesus knows all that is going on. He turns and says, "Suffer little children, and forbid them not, to come unto me : for of such is the kingdom of heaven." Then he takes them up in his arms and blesses them. The kingdom of heaven is for the little ones as well as for grown people. It is as much for poor children as for rich kings and queens.*

How joyful must those have been who thus took the children to Jesus ! What delight they must have felt when they saw him put his hands on their heads, and

* Matthew xix. 13—15 ; Mark x 13—16 ; Luke xviii. 15—17.

bless them ! And surely there is nothing that pious friends so much wish for their dear children as that they should come to Jesus. They have often told you of his love : will you not choose him for your Saviour and your Lord ?

At another time it was not like what you have now read. There were parents who would not let him bless their little ones. There were men and women with their children who did not believe on him. They were ready to cast

him out, and kill him.   Then he
looked on the city where they
dwelt, and wept.   As the tears
flowed down his face, he said that
he would have gathered them as
a hen gathers her chickens under
her wings, but they would not.*
How sad, that they all, both parents and children, would not
come to Jesus !

One of the first things he did
after he rose from the dead was to
tell one of his disciples to take care

* Matthew xxiii. 37-—39.

of the young. He said, " Feed my lambs." Notice the kind way in which he speaks. Not the lambs, but MY LAMBS. Those whom I love, who belong to my flock—my little ones.*

These stories of the love and tender care of Jesus for children come to us from years long past ; but they are ever new and sweet to us. He knew that the souls of children were of more value than all the silver, and gold, and

* John xxi. 15.

u

jewels that were in the world. He knew that their souls might be lost. He knew that he could save them ; that they might be happy now, and happy with him in heaven, and he said, " Suffer the little children to come unto me."

A little girl, only six or seven years old, was dying. Her eldest sister sat by her side with a Bible in her hand. " Read to me about Jesus blessing little children," said the dear child. The verses were then read, and the book was closed. " Oh, how kind," she said. " I shall soon go to Jesus. He will soon take me in his arms, and bless me too. No one will keep me away from him in heaven."

Her sister then kissed her, and said, " Do you love me?" " Yes, dear," she replied, " but, do not be angry, I love Jesus best."

It was right. Others had loved her ; but Jesus had died for her. Young reader, love your father and mother, love all around you, but be sure that you love Jesus more than all the rest.

" Forbid them not," the Saviour cried,
  " Let children in my blessings share;
My love can never be denied
  To such as need my special care."

Then in his kind enfolding arms,
  Children enjoyed his tender love;
Heard his mild voice, that voice which charms
  The saints below, and blest above.

Rejoice, ye children, rich and poor,
  For, lo! his smiles to you extend:
Receive his words; then love, adore,
  Your nearest, dearest, kindest Friend.

BETHANY.

VI. CHILDREN MAY NOW GO TO JESUS.

"I LOVE THEM THAT LOVE ME, AND THOSE
THAT SEEK ME EARLY SHALL FIND ME."—
Proverbs viii. 17.

JESUS still lives. He rose from
the dead, and is now in our nature
in heaven. He still invites little
children to come to him. He is
very near to them by his Spirit.
He can hear what they say. He
knows all they think.

He is not now going from
place to place, as when he was on
the earth. But he is by his

Spirit everywhere. He is now, and ever will be, the Lover of children. He still says to the young, "I love them that love me, and those that seek me early shall find me."

The words, "Suffer little children to come unto me," are put in the Bible for you. He had them written and printed for you to read. It is as if he spoke them to you, and to every little child.

The Lord Jesus now calls you by your parents, when they talk to you about your soul, and God, and heaven. He calls you by teachers and ministers when they speak to you of the blessed gospel. He calls you, it is hoped, by this little book, when you read it, or when it is read to you. He wants you to love him now, while your eyes are bright, and your cheeks have the bloom of health.

The call is made to you as children. He speaks to you as those who are very young in years, who know but little, and who cannot do much for him.

Jesus does not want you to talk

as grown-up people, or to act in all things like them. Early piety will not make you little men and women. It will not turn the tiny bud all at once into the full-blown flower. It will not change the small twig into a strong tree. You may run about and play. You may be happy all day long.

But it will make you humble, gentle, and loving. It will teach you to obey those who are over you. It will lead you to be kind to everybody. You will love to pray. You will do all things to please Jesus, just as his little ones should do. You will cling to him as your Saviour, with the simple love and faith of a child's heart.

How are you to obey his call? How can you come to him?

First, YOU CAN THINK ABOUT HIM. There was once a child who was far away from his father. His name was Frank. He was born in the hot country called India. His dear mother was dead, and so were three little brothers, who used to play with him. Frank was the only one left to his father, and very dearly did that father love him.

After some time Frank was taken ill. No care or love could make the roses bloom on his pale face. The doctor said that if he did not leave India he would die. This was sad news to his father. So to save his life, the father's darling boy was sent to England.

A lady took charge of Frank, for the father could not leave India. As they sailed in a ship the poor boy was very sad in his heart. He used to sit in a corner of the vessel, and weep.

There was an old sailor on board the ship who pitied the little pale child. He would often sit down with him and tell him nice stories. He spoke about the great deep sea, and storms, and far-off lands, and many other things. Then Frank told the sailor of his great trouble, and that he feared he should never see his father again.

The old man tried to comfort the little boy. He said that if he truly loved his father, he might fancy that he was nigh to him all the day long. He could do everything he had taught him to do just as if his eye were upon him. He might say the prayers and the hymns his father had taught him as if he were with him. He could do all things as if he heard his voice, and felt his soft kiss on his cheek.

And Frank found the old sailor's words true. During that long voyage he used to sit alone and think of his father. It almost seemed as if his father were with him, and spoke to him. Then he was happy when he began to enjoy what he called "heart visits to papa." It was then he found that those who really love one another may meet in thought, and feel as if they were once more with each other.

After this manner we may go to Jesus. He is not to be seen with our eyes, but we may take delight in thinking of him. We may think of what he did and said, and how he lived and died for us. "Coming to Jesus," then, is to think of him with trust: it is to have the desire of the heart towards him.

2. YOU CAN SPEAK TO JESUS. If he were on earth, as he once was, you could go to him. But then you would have to travel many, many miles. You would have to cross wide seas. It would, perhaps, take many weeks or months to get to him. The journey would take much time, and cost much money. And when

you came to where he was, you might have to push your way through a crowd of people. There also might be some who would keep you back, as it was in the old times.

But without all this trouble you can come to Jesus now. You are really better off than those who lived when he was on the earth. He is always within your call. You have not to go over the hills or across the deep waters, or from city to city, to find him. He is very near to you. He hears the

I

softest call. He knows all you want and all you wish.

Have you seen the wires raised on posts, at the side of the railroad? They go along for many miles. They pass over the hills and across the valleys. In some places they are carried under the water, from one land to another. People who have never seen each other, and who live hundreds of miles apart, can talk by the use of these wires. They can send messages by them. As soon as a wire is made, as it were, to speak at one end, it is heard at the other end. Almost as quickly as you think the message is carried along to a place afar off.

Is not this a great wonder? But it is not so great a wonder as prayer. The prayer of a little child on earth is heard in heaven at the very moment it is spoken. And in the same moment an answer may be given.

It is a great thing to speak to Jesus. He is the King of kings and Lord of all. Angels bow before him. All who are in heaven serve him. But if we pray with the heart he will be sure to hear us.

A lady once asked a little deaf and dumb girl, by writing on a slate, "What is prayer?" Now this little dumb girl, of course, had never said a prayer, for she could not speak; and she had never heard a prayer, for she was quite deaf. Yet you will find that she well knew what prayer is. She took the pencil, and wrote on the slate this reply: "Prayer is the wish of the heart."

" Do you pray, William? " said a teacher to a little boy who often did what he ought not to do. " Yes, sir," replied William, " I say my prayers twice every day." " But are you quite sure that you pray, or do you only repeat some words that you have been taught to use? I think, my dear boy, that if you truly prayed you would not be so cross and sullen. You would do what your parents wish you to do. You would be humble and loving, and not proud and un- kind. You would love to speak the truth. Ask Jesus to give you his grace, that you may turn from all sin, and may obey him in every duty."

Prayer, then, is the wish and desire of the heart. This is the prayer that Jesus loves. For fine words do not make true prayer if we do not feel what we say. But if we truly say, "Jesus, have mercy upon me; Lord, help a little child; Jesus, save me from all sin," this will be prayer, and so praying we shall be coming to him.

3. You can believe in Jesus. Perhaps you are not old enough to know what it is to believe, and what faith is. The sweet rose does not know how the dews of the night and the rain refresh it. The lily, that catches a few of the bright beams of the sun, does not know how they help to make it grow. But the dew and the rain and the sun do refresh the flowers, and make them what they are. So a child may not be able to know much about faith, and yet it may be in his

heart, and he may be a Christian child.

If your papa or mamma promise to do anything for you, you believe them. If they tell you that they will take you on a visit, you trust their word. You have faith in them, and you are quite sure that they mean what they say. They always speak the truth, and you know that they love you too well for them not to do what they promise. And in the same way you can believe the words and promises of Jesus.

You can rely on what he tells you in the Bible. You can trust in him as the Saviour of sinners.

One night a house was on fire. The smoke and flames rose up very high. The family rushed out of the door, all but a little boy. In his fright he ran up stairs, and soon was seen at a window. The poor fellow cried aloud for help. His father missed him. He looked up, and then heard his cries. "Throw yourself into my arms, my dear boy," he called to him: "I will catch you."

"Oh, I cannot see you, father."

"But I can see you, my child. Be quick, jump now."

Then the smoke grew more thick, and the fire was fast reaching the poor child. He stood for a moment, and with a bold spring threw himself from the window, and in an instant was in his father's arms. Do you not see that he had faith in his father?

We are all in danger of being lost—lost for ever—lost through sin. But Jesus can save us. He can save us now. He will save us if we cast our souls on him. He must, for there is no one else who can save us.

Come, then, like Mary, whom we read of in the Gospel, and sit at his feet. Come, like John, his disciple, and lean on his bosom. Come, like the children of old, and cry, " Hosanna : save, Lord, we pray thee." Like the little boy who threw himself into his father's arms, cast yourself by faith on Jesus.

We will now tell you of another

little boy—of one who looked to Jesus—who had faith in him.

This child, when four years old, was very much burnt. His clothes took fire. As he grew older he often was kept to his bed for three, four, or six months at a time. He was very weak, and mostly full of pain. His great comfort was to go to a Sunday-school when he was able. He used to go there on crutches. He loved his school, and was one of the best boys in it.

But he got so bad that he could not walk there, even on his

crutches. Some kind lads then got a little cart, and used to call for him; and in this way he was carried to his Sunday-school.

At last he got so much worse, that he could not go at all, and he was kept to his bed—a poor, sick boy.

You will be glad to know that he had been led by the Holy Spirit to believe in Jesus. Though he was so very ill, he was quite happy. His heart was full of love to the Saviour.

When he got any rest for his

body, or when anything was done for him, or given to him, he would say, "I thank Jesus for that help."

About a week before he died, his teacher asked him if he had any word to send to the school. He smiled, and said, "Tell them to mind what you say. Ask them to be at the school as often as they can. And tell them to look to Jesus."

These words, "Look to Jesus," were often on his lips. He had looked to him, and was happy;

and he wished every one to do so, that they might be happy too.

When he was dying, his teacher went to see him again. He found him with his eyes closed, and he seemed fast sinking. His mother bent over him, and asked if he had anything to say to his teacher. Yes, he had some words to speak: they were these—" Look to Jesus," he said, with a soft, weak voice.

The last words he spoke were to a little girl named Ellen, who had often called to sing to him. And what were those words? They were the same he had so often spoken, and which had given joy to his own heart: " LOOK TO JESUS."

Soon after this he went to be with the Saviour in whom he trusted, and whom he loved.

Young children once to Jesus came,
  His blessing to entreat;
And I may humbly do the same
  Before his mercy seat.

If babes so many years ago
  His tender pity drew,
He will not surely let me go
  Without a blessing too.

SILOAM.

"LEARN OF ME.—FOLLOW ME."—*Matt.* xi. 29; *Luke* ix. 59.

EVERY little boy should have a good copy before him when he is learning to write. A good pattern is what every little girl wishes to have when she is trying to do a piece of fancy work. If we have to take a long journey in a strange, dark road, it is well for us to have a guide that we may safely follow. But then, it is much more need-ful that we should have a good example, a pattern, and a guide for our conduct in life.

We have many examples in the Bible. Some are for the young, and others for the old, and some for all sorts of people. Many are of those who lived in wicked times. They shine like stars in a dark sky. But there is one example which shines like the bright sun in all its glory.

Jesus is the best example. He is a lovely pattern of what even the youngest child should be. We may safely follow him. If we love him, we shall be like him ; for we are almost sure to copy those we love.

Let us now find out some of the ways in which a child should be like Jesus. You have already heard of the HOLY CHILD,* that he obeyed his mother. He has shown you, by his example, that you must do all you can to honour your parents, and to make their hearts glad. For piety towards them is the next thing to piety towards God. It will be for you

* Page 35.

now to see in what other ways you may take him as a pattern.

1. JESUS WAS MEEK. He said, "I am meek and lowly in heart."* To be meek is to be humble, and not to think too much of yourself. It is to be gentle and kind when you cannot have your own way. It is to speak loving words when others speak unkind ones. It is to give up your own will that others may be made happy. It is not to fret and murmur when others hurt or offend you. It is

* Matthew xi. 29.

to do all things in a quiet and gentle spirit and manner.

Jesus was always meek. He never spoke an angry word. He was meek when a child, and meek when a man. When they called him ill names, when they struck him with their hands, when they tried to kill him by throwing him down a high hill, he bore all meekly. When they would not believe his words, and when they mocked him because he said he was the Son of God, he did not speak an angry word. "When he was reviled, he reviled not again."*

2. JESUS WAS FORGIVING. — One day Peter came to him, and said, "Lord, how often shall my brother offend against me, and I forgive him? Till seven times?" Peter thought it would be a great thing to forgive any one seven times. He might forgive once or twice ; but it was hard to forgive any one seven times. Then Jesus said unto him, "I say not unto thee, Until seven times, but, until seventy times seven."†

---

* 1 Peter ii. 23.　　　† Matthew xviii. 22.

You know what he has taught you to say in his prayer—the Lord's prayer. You are to be forgiven as you forgive others. He says that if we do not forgive, God will not have mercy on us. We are not to wait till people ask for it, but we are to do it at once, and with all our heart.

And he gave us an example of it. When they spat on him, and when they flogged him on the back with whips, love was in his heart. When they nailed him to the cross, he prayed, saying,

"Father, forgive them, for they know not what they do."* Such was the lovely spirit of Jesus.

A boy struck a little Irish lad in school time. The master saw the blow given, and he called the boy to stand up to be flogged. The Irish lad then said, "Oh, sir, do not whip him. Pray forgive him." "Why do you wish that I should not punish him?" the master asked. "Because, sir, I have read that Jesus forgave those who struck him, and he said that

* Luke xxiii. 34.

we must also forgive those who hurt us." Surely that Irish lad had taken Jesus for an example.

When some Hindoo lads read for the first time these words of Jesus, " I say unto you, Love your enemies, bless them that curse you,"* one of them cried aloud, " Oh, how lovely!" For some time after he was still heard to say, " Oh, how good! how fine! Surely this must be the truth."

If everybody now loves you, and is kind, you think that they

* Matthew v. 44.

will always be kind and loving.
But you may find some people
who do not talk and act as they
should. Some may say unkind
words about you, and others may
try to hurt you. Then it will be
for you to think of Jesus, and
follow his example. Forgive all
who do you evil.

3. JESUS LOVED PRAYER. —
Though he was the Son of God,
he prayed. Though he did no
sin, he prayed. After he had
been all day doing good, and was
weary, he went to a hill and spent

all night in prayer. He asked his Father, perhaps, that his body might be strong to do the great work he had come to do. He prayed for his church—for those he had come to save.

If Jesus prayed, should not we do so? We who are so dark in our minds, and are so full of sin: we who are so weak, and have so many wants. Yes, we ought to pray.

Just as a child who loves his parents will love to speak to them, so those who love God will pray to him. We must tell God that we are sorry for our sin. We must ask him to forgive us, for the sake of Jesus Christ. We must beg of him to give us his Holy Spirit, to make us holy. We must pray for all things we want. We must pray for all those we love ; and if there are any who are not kind to us, we must ask God to bless them also.

4. JESUS WAS HOLY. — He always did what was right. He never did any evil. Not one sin was committed by him. He was

quite pure. No wrong word, or thought, or deed ever stained his soul. He always did right from a right MOTIVE. It was because he felt rightly, that he did what was good. He was tempted by Satan to do evil, but he would not do it. He came to keep his Father's law for his people's sakes. They had broken it, but he came to honour it; and he did it for those who believe in him.

You can never be holy as he was, for you have a sinful heart. But you must try to be like him, and ask God to give you his grace, that you may be like him as far as you can be. You cannot do all he did when he grew up to be a man. You cannot heal the sick, nor give sight to the blind; but you can help to make home a happy place, and be of use in the world. You can obey a rule or law which he gave us, and which he always obeyed himself, "Do unto others as you would that they should do unto you."* This is called "The Golden

* Luke vi. 31.

Rule." If you attend to it, you may become more like the holy child Jesus.

You have now heard that Jesus was meek, forgiving, prayerful, and holy.

There are other ways in which he is your Pattern and Example; but we cannot tell you of them now. If you seek to follow him in those things of which you have been told, you will soon learn what the rest are.

One word more. It will not do for you to say that you WISH

you were like him. You must TRY to be like him. You will say when you do anything, Is it such as I ought to do? Is it such as will please Jesus? Is it such as will make me more like him? You will say, O Lord, help me to be meek, gentle, kind, and dutiful, that I may be like thee.

TIBERIAS.

THREE times did Jesus ask
Peter, " Lovest thou me ? "
Three times did Peter reply,
" Lord, thou knowest that I love
thee." And now we ask you,
Do you love Jesus ?

You like to hear about him.
You are glad when papa or mamma tell you some of the true
stories of his grace. That is quite
right ; but do you LOVE him ?

You have your own Bible, in which you read about him every day. We are happy to know that too; but do you LOVE him?

Perhaps you say that you can speak about him, and can repeat a great many texts by heart. You have often spoken to your young friends of Jesus the Saviour. That is again good; but do you LOVE him?

There are some children who give some of their pennies to the mission-box; or who collect money from others, that the Bible and tracts may be sent to the heathen. If you are one of these, you do well. Let the name of Jesus be known through all the world; but do you LOVE him?

Our Lord Jesus Christ asks for your love. He has the best right to the best place in your heart. It is a great sin not to love him. If you give him your heart, it will be the best thing you have done, or can do. You will be glad of it as long as you live. It will make you happy for ever and ever.

Jesus says, "Ye shall seek me,

and find me, when ye shall search for me with all your heart."* And there never will come a better time to seek and love than now. It may be, if you do not love him while you are young, you may never love him at all.

Why do we speak in such a way? It is because we cannot forget the great love of Jesus towards us. He became poor for our sakes. He bore our sins in his own body on the tree. All who shall be saved have been

* Jeremiah xxix. 13.

bought with a price of more value than all the riches of the world. The price was not silver and gold, but "the precious blood of Christ."*

We so speak to you because we know that you will not trust in him as your Saviour, unless you love him. You will not seek to be like him, unless you love him. You will not truly repent before God, unless you love Jesus.

Now think of the many favours you enjoy, and which others do

* 1 Peter i. 18.

not.   Think of your happy home,
your kind parents, your Bible and
pretty books, and then hear Jesus,
who has given them all, say unto
you, " Lovest thou me ?"

Think of some poor black boy.
He was born in Africa.   He is
taught to bow down to an ugly
image, made of clay, and to call
it his god.   When he sees a ser-
pent he prays to it.   He grows
up in the ways of sin, and has no
kind teacher to lead him in the
path to heaven.

See   that   little   Hindoo   girl.

She is ten years old. She does
not go to any school. In the part
of the land where she lives there
is no school for girls. Her father
says she has no soul, and he feels
no love for her. She is left to
grow up like the beasts that perish.
If she prays at all, it is to a block
of wood or stone.

Look at your happy state, and
then at the state of poor heathen
boys and girls. In your home
how many things there are to
make you happy. Then turn to
the homes of many of those far

away. Their houses are of mud walls. There are no chairs, or tables, or beds. All sit on the ground; and if they have a mat they sit by day and sleep at night upon it.

A poor heathen child falls ill, but has not the comforts you have at such a time. And if it should die, the parents beat their breasts and tear their hair; but they have no good hope of meeting again in a better world.

You, then, are not like these heathen children. God has been very kind to you in placing you where he is known, and giving you so many of his loving gifts for the body and the soul.

Now, what can you do to show your love to him ? Jesus does not expect a child that loves him to do great things, but little things. Kind words and gentle deeds are the fruits he seeks to find on the young plants of grace : just those things which a child may and ought to do.

You shall hear of what a little girl did. She was in a mission school in Ceylon. First, she gave her heart to the Lord, and then she tried to lead others to know him. But her great concern was for the soul of her poor mother, who still bowed down to idols.

The mother lived a good many miles from the school, and the girl used often to go to visit her. Once when she went to the hut, her mother spread a mat on the ground for her to sit upon. Then she went to boil some rice for her child.

The little girl said, " I am not hungry, mother.   I do not want anything to eat, but I want very much to talk to you."

" Well," said the mother, "you can do that when I have got the rice ready."   The people mostly live on rice in that land.

The girl again said that she did not want any food.   She had come to speak about Jesus, and to beg of her to throw away her false gods.   "Oh ! mother, I love you, and long that your soul may be saved."

"If you speak against my gods," said the mother, "I will beat you."

"Dear mother, if you do beat me, I must tell you of Jesus;" and then she wept.

The mother now felt that her child must love her, or she would not talk to her in such a way. So she sat down by her side, and heard her child speak about the Saviour.

It was not long after this time before the parent was led to give up her idol gods, and to live as a Christian.

You have now seen how a little
girl in a heathen land showed
her love to Jesus.   " Even a child
is known by his doings."*   It
was a great work she tried, and a
great work she did.   But love
makes hard things easy.

———

Now you have come to the end
of the book.   But before we say
" good-by," we must first pray
that God would grant you his
Holy Spirit, so that you may give
your heart to Jesus now.   May

* Proverbs xx. 11.

M

you love Jesus all the days you live on the earth. Then you will live with him in heaven. It will be your happy home. There will be no more sorrow, no more crying, no more death, because there will be no more sin. Pride and ill-nature cannot enter there. All shall be pure and holy and happy for ever.

Yes, heaven is full of love. God is love. The saints dwell in love. All are loving and lovely. Will you not, then, love and serve Jesus on earth, that you may be

with them, and have a white robe
and a crown of glory in heaven?

Around the throne of God in heaven
  Thousands of children stand;
Children whose sins are all forgiven,
  A holy, happy band,
      Singing glory, glory, glory.

Once they were little things like you,
  And lived on earth below,
And could not praise, as now they do,
  The Lord who loved them so;
      Singing glory, glory, glory.

What brought them to that world above,
  That heaven so bright and fair;
Where all is peace, and joy, and love?
  How came those children there?
      Singing glory, glory, glory.

Because the Saviour shed his blood
  To take away their sin;
Washed in that pure and precious flood,
  Behold them white and clean,
      Singing glory, glory, glory.

On earth they sought the Saviour's grace,
  On earth they loved his name;
So now they see his blessed face,
  And stand before the Lamb,
      Singing glory, glory, glory.

Reed and Pardon, Printers, Paternoster Row.

PUBLICATIONS

OF THE

RELIGIOUS TRACT SOCIETY.

CHILDREN'S BOOKS.

THE PICTURE SCRAP BOOK;

Or, Happy Hours at Home. In two Parts. A Selection of superior Engravings, suited alike to the Parlour, Nursery, and School Room. Royal 4to, finely printed on Tinted Paper. Each part complete in itself, 4s. in cover; or bound together, gilt edges, 8s.

BOOK OF SUNDAY PICTURES FOR LITTLE CHILDREN.

OLD TESTAMENT. Beautiful coloured Pictures in Oil Colours, and Wood Engravings. In fancy cover, gilt edges, 3s.

BOOK OF SUNDAY PICTURES.

NEW TESTAMENT. With beautiful coloured Pictures in Oil Colours, and numerous Wood Engravings. In fancy cover, gilt edges, 3s.

CHILDREN OF THE BIBLE.

With superior coloured Engravings. Small 4to, 2s. elegant cover.

GRANDMAMMA WISE;

Or, Visits to Rose Cottage. With Three beautiful coloured Engravings. 18mo, 1s. 6d. cloth boards; 2s. extra boards, gilt edges.

MY POETRY BOOK.

With Three beautiful coloured Engravings. 18mo, 1s. 6d. cloth boards; 2s. extra boards, gilt edges.

KATIE SEYMOUR;

Or, How to make Others Happy. 18mo. Three coloured Engravings, 1s. 6d. cloth boards; 2s. extra boards, gilt edges.

A BOOK ABOUT ANIMALS.

Coloured Engravings. Small 4to, 2s. in fancy cover.

A BOOK ABOUT BIRDS.

Coloured Engravings. Small 4to, 2s. in fancy covers.

THE HISTORY OF MOSES.

Coloured Engravings. 1s. in fancy covers.

2

THE HISTORY OF JOSEPH AND HIS BRETHREN.

Coloured Engravings. 1s. in fancy covers.

THE HISTORY OF RUTH.

Coloured Engravings. 1s. in fancy covers.

THE HISTORY OF SAMUEL.

Coloured Engravings. 1s. in fancy covers.

THE PRETTY VILLAGE.

Coloured Engravings. 1s. in fancy covers.

VISITS TO HOLLY FARM.

Coloured Engravings. 1s. in fancy covers.

NEW SHORT STORIES.

In Packets, each containing Sixteen Books, price 6d. Neatly printed and illustrated, stitched in coloured fancy wrappers, and enclosed in a gilt envelope.

MY BOX OF BOOKS.

Ornamented Box, containing one each of the above New Short Stories. Price 1s. 6d.

It will be found a very novel and acceptable Gift to a Child.

3

THE LITTLE LIBRARY.

Containing Thirty-two Books suited for Little Children, in an Ornamented Box.   Price 1s.

THE CHILD'S BOOKCASE.

A Fancy Box containing 32 interesting Books, price 1s.

PICTURE BOOKS FOR LITTLE CHILDREN.

Assorted 8d. per Dozen.

Every page has a good Engraving.   The set may be had complete in an Ornamented Case, price 1s.   Adapted as a Present to a Child.

PICTURE CARDS.

PICTURE CARDS ILLUSTRATIVE OF THE PILGRIM'S PROGRESS.

Packet I.   CHRISTIAN.—Twelve large Cards, beautifully printed in Oil Colours, with Letterpress Description.   1s. per Packet.

Packet II.   CHRISTIANA AND HER CHILDREN.—Ditto, 1s. per Packet.

EMBOSSED PICTURE CARDS.

Beautifully printed in Oil Colours, and suited for Rewards in Families and Schools.

A PACKET containing 16 sorts, in ornamented wrapper, 1s.

The CHILD'S PACKET, ditto, ditto, 1s.

GOOD CONDUCT CARDS.

A Packet of 12 ornamented Cards, beautifully printed in Oil Colours and designed for Rewards, 6d.

BOOKS FOR THE YOUNG.

ARNOLD LESLIE;

Or, A Working Man's Experience. 18mo. 1s. 6d. cloth boards.

BRIGHTNESS AND BEAUTY;

Or, The Religion of Christ affectionately recommended to the Young. By the Rev. E. MANNERING. 18mo, 1s. cloth boards; 1s. 6d. half-bound.

CHILD'S BOOK OF POETRY.

Original and Selected. Engravings. 18mo, 1s. 6d. cloth boards, neat.

FRANK NETHERTON;

Or, The Talisman. Engravings. 18mo, 1s. 6d. cloth boards; 2s. extra boards.

GILBERT GRESHAM.

18mo. With Engravings. 1s. 6d. cloth boards; 2s. extra boards.

HANNAH LEE;

Or, Rest for the Weary. 18mo. With Engravings. 1s. 6d. cloth boards; 2s. extra boards, gilt edges.

HISTORICAL TALES FOR YOUNG PROTESTANTS.

With Engravings. Royal 18mo, 2s. cloth boards; 2s. 6d. extra boards, gilt edges.

THE HIVE AND ITS WONDERS.

18mo. Engravings, 1s. cloth boards; 1s. 6d. extra boards, gilt edges.

LIFE'S MORNING;

Or, Counsels and Encouragements for Youthful Christians. By the Author of "Life's Evening," etc. 2s. cloth boards; 2s. 6d. extra boards, gilt edges.

LITTLE MAY;

Or, Of what Use am I ? Engravings. 1s. 6d. cloth boards : 2s. extra boards, gilt edges.

MARGARET CRAVEN;

Or, Beauty of the Heart. By the late Miss S. FRY. 18mo. Engravings. 1s. 6d. cloth boards; 2s. extra boards.

MAY COVERLEY, THE YOUNG DRESSMAKER.

18mo. With Engravings. 2s. cloth boards.

MIRACLES OF CHRIST;

With Explanatory Observations and Illustrations. 18mo. Engravings. 1s. 6d. cloth boards ; 2s. half-bound.

MISSIONARY BOOK FOR THE YOUNG.

A First Book on Missions. Engravings. 18mo. 1s. cloth ; 1s. 6d. cloth extra.

ORPHAN'S FRIEND.

Engravings. 32mo. 8d. cloth boards ; 1s. half bound.

THE EARTH'S RICHES;

Or, Underground Stores. By the Author of " Peeps at Nature," etc. Fcap. 8vo. 2s. 6d. cloth boards ; 3s. 6d. extra boards, gilt edges.

7

THE ENGLISH PEASANT GIRL.

18mo. With Engravings. 1s. 6d. cloth boards; 2s. extra boards, gilt edges.

THE LITTLE GUIDE OF ADRIGHOOLE.

Fcap. 8vo. Engravings. 2s. 6d. cloth boards; 3s. extra boards.

THE LOST KEY.

By the late Miss S. FRY. 18mo. Engravings. 1s. 6d. cloth boards; 2s. extra boards.

THE OBJECT OF LIFE.

Foolscap 8vo. With superior Engravings. 3s. cloth boards; 3s. 6d. extra boards.

THE STORY OF A POCKET BIBLE.

By the Author of " Gilbert Gresham," " Stories of School Boys," etc. Fcap. 8vo. With Engravings. 3s. 6d. boards; 4s. extra gilt.

THE YOUNG ENVELOPE MAKERS.

By the late Miss S. FRY. 18mo. Engravings. 1s. 6d. cloth boards; 2s. extra boards, gilt edges

8